DINOSAUR BOB

AND HIS ADVENTURES WITH THE FAMILY LAZARDO

WILLIAM JOYCE

HARPER & ROW, PUBLISHERS

Copyright © 1988 by William Joyce
Printed in the U.S.A. All rights reserved.
Typography by Cathryn S. Aison

Library of Congress Cataloging-in-Publication Data
Joyce, William.
   Dinosaur Bob and his adventures with the
family Lazardo/William Joyce.—1st ed.
      p.   cm.
   Summary: While vacationing in Africa, the
Lazardo family finds and brings back to Amer-
ica a friendly dinosaur that becomes the talk of
the town.
   ISBN 0-06-023047-9: $
   ISBN 0-06-023048-7 (lib. bdg.): $
   [1. Dinosaurs—Fiction.   2. Family life—Fic-
tion.]   I. Title.
PZ7.J857Di 1988   87-30796
[E]—dc19   CIP
                                      AC

          5   6   7   8   9   10

Special thanks to Nick and Nora Charles,
Mr. Kong, eighth wonder of the world,
and Matthew Welbourne, third nephew of mine.

Every year, before the start of the baseball season, the Lazardo family took a trip far from their home in Pimlico Hills. One afternoon, while on safari in Africa, young Scotty Lazardo wandered away from camp. He returned with a dinosaur.

"Look what I caught!" he said.

"Can we keep him?" pleaded Scotty's sisters, Zelda and Velma.

"I don't see why not," said Dr. Lazardo.

"He looks kind of like my uncle Bob," said Mrs. Lazardo.

Jumbu, their bodyguard, said nothing.

Scotty patted the dinosaur on the nose. "Bob?" he tried.

The dinosaur smiled and wagged his giant tail.

So they named him Bob.

With Bob along, safari life was fun: swimming in the mornings, games of baseball in the afternoons, and songs by the campfire before bed.

When it came time to start for home, the Lazardos couldn't stand the thought of leaving Bob behind.

"Would you like to come home with us, Bob?" asked Dr. Lazardo.

"We'd love to have you," said Mrs. Lazardo.

"You could play baseball for our home team, the Pimlico Pirates!" cried Scotty, Zelda, and Velma.

Bob smiled again and wagged his giant tail.

The journey back was grand. When the safari came to the banks of the river Nile, Dr. Lazardo said, "Let's go sailing!"

So they made Bob into a ship and steered him down the river.

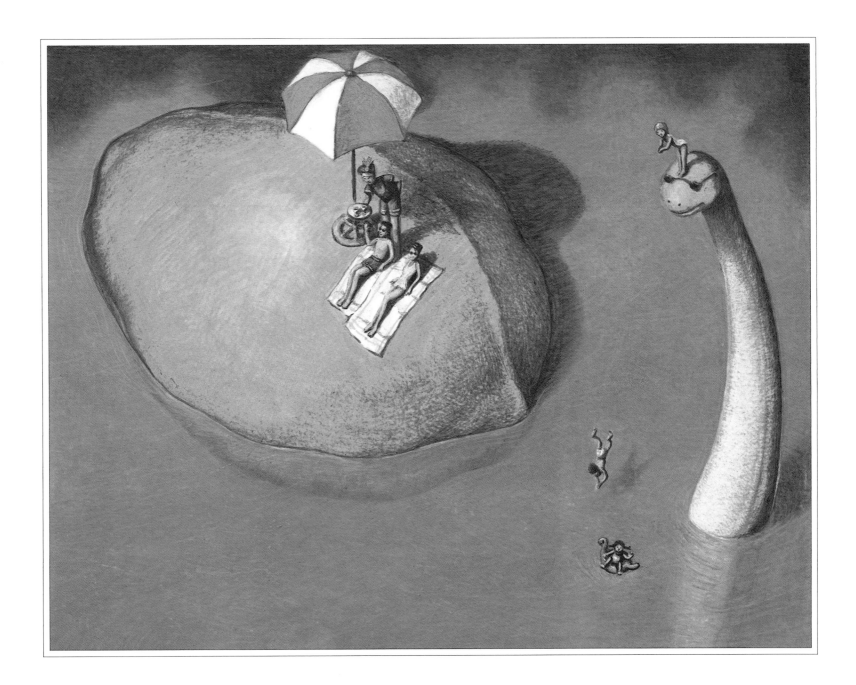

But they couldn't sail Bob all the way home to Pimlico Hills.
So Dr. Lazardo booked passage on a luxury liner.

"Bob took us down the Nile in style," reasoned the Doctor. "It
would be bad manners if we didn't return the favor."

It was a wonderful voyage! Passengers danced the conga up
and down Bob's back while he played his trumpet—a gift from
the ship's orchestra.

Every evening, the children led Bob up to his berth in the
ship's smokestacks and brought him a little bedtime snack—two
peanut-butter-and-bologna sandwiches and 400 double Dutch
chocolate cakes.

When the ship reached New York City, the Lazardos visited Central Park. After a light snack of 750 hot dogs, they caught a train to Pimlico Hills.

It was Bob's first train ride.

Reporters flocked to the Lazardo house in Pimlico Hills.

"Bob will scare off burglars," Dr. Lazardo told them.

"And he can blow a mean trumpet," said Zelda.

"He can dance, too," said Velma and Mrs. Lazardo at the same time.

"And can he play **baseball**!" shouted Scotty.

Jumbu said nothing.

The photographers' cameras flashed. LENGTHY LIZARD LANDS WITH LAZARDOS read the headline in the paper.

Bob was famous.

The next day, Bob and the Lazardos played some baseball in the backyard. Bob was terrific. He could play right and left field at the same time!

The Pimlico Pirates watched Bob play. The Pirates had never won a game. They were the worst team in history. But everyone in town loved them and went to all their games.

"I wish the big guy in green could play for us," said one of the Pirates.

The following morning, Bob saw some neighborhood dogs chasing cars. He decided to join them.

He was stopped by a policeman. "Aren't you the Lazardos' dinosaur?"

Bob nodded.

He was arrested for disturbing the peace.

Bob enjoyed being fingerprinted. He didn't understand he was in trouble.

The Lazardos rushed to get Bob out of prison. But the chief of police wouldn't let him go.

"I'm sorry," the chief explained. "We can't have dinosaurs running wild in the streets. We'll be sending him back to Africa in the morning."

Bob let out a sad howl. So did the Lazardos. Everyone—even the policemen—began to cry.

That night, no one at the Lazardos' house could sleep.

"Poor Bob," sighed Scotty.

"All alone," said Velma.

"Without his trumpet," said Zelda.

Suddenly, Dr. Lazardo jumped up, grabbed his hat, and ran out the door.

"Don't worry," said Mrs. Lazardo. "Your father never goes out in his pajamas unless he has a smashing idea."

Soon the Doctor returned with the Pimlico Pirates.

"Come on," he whispered, "and be very quiet. I think I know how to save Bob!"

Bob's escape made headlines the following morning:

LAZARDOS AND LIZARD ON THE LAM. COPS CONFUSED.

The people of Pimlico Hills weren't worried. They were too busy thinking about the Pirates' opening game. The whole town was going that afternoon, even the chief of police.

As the stadium filled, no one noticed a large bump in the outfield. The team began to run out onto the baseball diamond as the announcer called their names. When the last of the team was called, the announcer shouted, "...And now the newest Pimlico Pirate: DINOSAUR BOB!"

The bump began to move. There stood Bob!

The crowd roared. So did the chief of police!

Bob smiled his big dinosaur grin and the game began.

The game was close. The Lazardos cheered Bob from the dugout and gave him water between innings. The Pirates were playing better than they ever had. They needed just one run to win the game when Dinosaur Bob stepped up to bat. He swung with all his might. *CRACK!* The ball went up and up, clear out of the stadium and out of sight!

Bob rounded the bases in three great strides and touched his nose to home plate. The Pimlico Pirates had won the game!

The Lazardos rushed onto the field and hugged Bob. And the crowd cheered Bob all the way to the Lazardos' house. The chief of police cheered the loudest.

Bob was a hero.

That evening, Bob and the Lazardos celebrated by having a cookout in the backyard. After dinner, Jumbu brought out the musical instruments. Scotty on bongos, Bob on trumpet. And everyone else on kazoos.

"Here's to Bob," said Dr. and Mrs. Lazardo.

"The best ball player...," said Velma.

"The best pal...," said Zelda.

"And the best **dinosaur** a family ever had!" shouted Scotty.

Jumbu smiled.

And they all sang and danced late into the summer night.

the end